THE
EXTRAORDINARY
BUBBLE

THE
EXTRAORDINARY
BUBBLE

AND OTHER FANCIFUL ADVENTURE STORIES
Compiled by the Editors
of
Highlights for Children

CONTENTS

THE EXTRAORDINARY BUBBLE

By Katherine Jordan

Callie sat on the front steps, thinking hard.

"I want each of you to think of something extraordinary that has happened in your life," her teacher, Mr. McNeil, had said on Monday morning. "On Friday everyone will get a chance to tell a story."

Today was Thursday, and Callie still couldn't think of anything. She idly picked up her little sister's bottle of soap bubbles and rubbed her thumb up and down the side, trying to concentrate.

"Extra-ordinary," she mumbled. "That means out of the ordinary. I sure wish something out of the ordinary would happen to me!"

Suddenly, there was a sputter of smoke, and soap from the bottle splashed onto her hands. Before she had time to blink, a tattered-looking genie stood in front of her.

"Wait a minute!" Callie managed to gasp. "I thought you guys were supposed to come out of magic lamps!"

The genie shook his head tiredly. "When was the last time you saw one of those lamps?" he demanded. "These days, we genies have to make do with what we can get. And with all the plastic containers, it's not easy, believe me!"

"Does this mean I get three wishes?" Callie asked excitedly. "Let's see . . . first I'd like . . ."

"Now just hold on," interrupted the genie. "Times are tough right now. I can't even afford a decent turban any more. I'm afraid one wish is the limit. And if I'm not mistaken, you already made it."

Callie stared in surprise. "I did?"

The genie nodded firmly. "You wished for something extraordinary to happen, right? So here goes."

Before Callie had time to reply, a bubble began to emerge from the bottle. It got bigger and wider, until both she and the genie were sitting inside it.

"Hang on," the genie announced with a grin. "It's a windy day."

Then they were off. The bubble floated high over the school, Callie saw a few kids playing basketball. When the bubble swooped down past the library and whisked along the main streets of town, Callie saw people everywhere, going about their everyday business. No one seemed to notice the huge bubble.

"Why isn't anybody looking at us?" Callie asked breathlessly. The genie shrugged. "Probably because they've never seen anything like this before. It's hard to believe, but most people see only what they expect to."

Callie pressed her face against the smooth walls of the bubble. "It's like we're flying in a fishbowl," she said in amazement. "Are you sure this thing won't break?"

The genie nodded. "As long as we stay away from the TV antennas and tall trees, we'll be fine. I've been hanging out in soap-bubble bottles for quite a while now, so I've had plenty of practice with this little trick."

"Do a lot of people wish for something like this?" asked Callie.

"For something extraordinary? All the time." The genie leaned back against the side of the bubble.

"The funny part of it is, this is pretty ordinary stuff for a genie. What's *really* extraordinary are the things you take for granted."

"Like what?" Callie asked.

The genie waved his hand at the streets below. "Like a house you can always come home to. A family and friends to share it with . . ." He rubbed a patched sleeve across his eyes.

Callie stared at the houses beneath them. "Maybe I should be getting back," she said quietly. Without a word, the genie waved his arms, and the bubble sailed softly down onto Callie's front steps again. Then suddenly it was gone.

"I guess it's time to climb back into the bottle," sighed the genie.

Callie shook her head. "Wait a minute. My mom has an old vase on the mantelpiece in the living room. It's not exactly a magic lamp, but it might be more comfortable than . . ."

"Say no more," the genie declared. He reached into the little plastic bottle and pulled out a bulging duffel bag. "I always travel light," he said with a wink. "Just show me the way!"

The next day Callie arrived home from school and flopped down on the living room sofa. "How did your speech go?" her mother inquired, dust-cloth in hand.

"OK, I guess," Callie answered. "I'm not sure anybody believed it, but they all liked my story."

"Sounds like it went pretty well to me," said her mother. "Now if only I could get this old vase to shine a little," she mumbled, rubbing the cloth vigorously against it.

Callie leaped to her feet. "Mom, wait . . . !"

Boggart's Flitting

By Judy Cox

"THUMP! WHUMP! CRASH!" The usual sounds
came from downstairs, letting George know it was
time to get up. Better than any rooster, the boggart was. The farmer pushed the blanket away
with his feet and began to get dressed. Downstairs, he knew he'd find a mess of broken crock-
ery, spilled flour, and soured milk, just as he had
every morning since the boggart moved in.

His wife, Maggie, sat up in bed. "I tell you,
George, I won't have it!" she scolded. "Not another

minute will I stay in this house with a boggart! A haunted house, yes. Give me a nice quiet, gentle old lady ghost who appears once in a blue moon. But a boggart? No! I'm telling you, George, you must do something about it!"

"CRASH!" came from downstairs.

"And if that's my new china pitcher that I bought from Meg McDonald on Friday last—well then, George, it's him or me!" Maggie said as she glared at her husband.

George sighed, laced up his boots, and went downstairs to clean up the damage.

Redtop Farm had been a peaceful place for nearly four hundred years. As in his Da's and Granda's time before him, George milked the cows, slopped the pigs, mowed the hay, and collected the eggs. All had been fine.

Until last May, when the boggart moved in.

George knew about boggarts, of course. A lot of old country places had a household spirit or goblin. Why, just down the swale, the Watson farm was quite well known for its boggart. George decided to pay the Watsons a visit.

He found Jamey Watson in the barn, feeding his horses. "Our boggart?" he said, after George told his story. "Oh, yes, been here for years. Quite a helpful chap, actually. Milks the cows, feeds the hens. Once he even saddled up Bess for me!" Jamey laughed and slapped his mare on the neck. "Musta been something to see, eh? Tack floating through the air?" George sighed. His boggart was not a helpful fellow at all.

He returned home to find his wife in a state. She sliced the bread in a fury, flinging the pieces upon a platter. "I put the baby down for a nap," she told him angrily. "And when I was certain she was asleep, I went outside to bring in the wash."

"But the boggart had been there," George said.

"Of course!" she cried. "The clean clothes were knocked all about in the dirt. When I went in to the baby, I found her sound asleep on the floor near the cradle. And you won't be telling me that a tiny wee thing only three months old climbed out by herself and covered herself up with her own woolly blankie, now will you!?"

Maggie poured the tea from the kettle, not caring where it splashed. "It's the last straw," she told George, setting the cups and saucers down on the table so hard they rattled. "It's home to Mother I'm going, and I won't be back until you get rid of that boggart!"

George took a long sip of tea. Always a quiet man, he was nearly morose when thinking. And he was thinking now.

"The boggart up at Jamey Watson's hall is a different sort," he told his wife reflectively. "Shame we couldn't tame ours, like. You know, gentle it down some. Maybe it only needs to be useful?" He set his teacup down.

His wife stood, her hands on her hips. "Well, you let me know when you tame it." she said. "Baby and I will be at Mother's."

Maggie left with the baby the next day. George waved good-bye until the cart was out of sight. Then he went back in and cleaned up the rancid butter the boggart had smeared on the table the night before.

For a week things were the same. George woke to the sounds of the boggart's mischief, and, in addition to his chores, tried to keep house. The work was hard and the boggart's tricks made it harder. Finally he could stand no more.

One day, so early in the morning the stars still burned in the heavens, George loaded up his cart with the chairs, tables, beds, and chests that had been in the house for four hundred years. He meant to get clean away without the boggart's ever knowing what happened.

Jamey Watson came up just as he finished tying down the load. "You're off, then?" Jamey asked, lighting his pipe.

"Aye," George said. "The boggart may have the place. 'Tis tired of his tricks I am. My wife and *bairn* have left. Now I'll be going, too."

From the top of the cart came a new voice, right out of the thin, chilly air. A rough voice, a sly voice. "Aye, Jamey, we're flitting." Both men looked. There was no one there.

Jamey blew out a cloud of pipe smoke. "Best you stay," he said. "A boggart in his own home is easier to live with than a boggart somewhere new. Give it a saucer of warm milk every night and a pillow by the fire to sleep on, and see if you don't make a new boggart of it."

George tried Jamey's advice. In a week it was milking the cows. In two weeks it was feeding the hens. In three it was washing the dishes, pretty as you please. By the end of the month, Maggie moved back home.

And, after that, George always bragged that he had the gentlest, most helpful of boggarts in the whole county.

The Monster in Meredith's Dream

By Eileen Spinelli

For three nights Meredith had a bad dream.
A monster was chasing her.

Meredith told her mother about the monster, and her mother had a suggestion: "Think of pleasant things before you go to sleep." So Meredith did.

She climbed under the covers and thought of her favorite place, the beach. She imagined the warm brown sand, the delicate pink seashells, and the blue-green water splashing about her ankles. Soon she was fast asleep.

That night Meredith did dream of the beach.

But the monster was there, chasing her through the foaming surf.

The following night, Mother had another suggestion: "Keep your bedside lamp on all night." So Meredith did.

She climbed under the covers and closed her eyes against the light. As usual, the monster appeared. Only now it was worse. In the light, its face was easier to see—and more frightening than ever.

This time Meredith's mother suggested music. "Keep your radio on," she said. So Meredith did.

She climbed under the covers and hummed along with the music and tapped her toes against the sheets until she fell asleep.

That night the monster *danced* in Meredith's dream. It wasn't a very good dance, and what's more, being danced after by a monster is not much better than being chased.

Meredith's mother sighed. "I'm running out of ideas." She thought for a while. "Except for one last thing you can try."

"What is it?" Meredith begged, anxious to be done with her scary monster dreams.

"Make friends with the monster," Mother said.

"What?!" Meredith screeched. "How do I do that?"

Meredith's mother smiled. "When the monster begins to chase you, don't run."

"Don't run?" squealed Meredith.

"That's right. Instead of running, turn around. Face that old monster and say, 'Hello! My name is Meredith. What's yours?'" Meredith wasn't at all sure she could do it. But she agreed to try.

That night she climbed under the covers and closed her eyes. Soon she was fast asleep. . . .

The next morning Meredith's mother heard noises in the kitchen. *Meredith must be fixing breakfast,* she thought. So she put on her robe and went downstairs.

There in the kitchen—as cozy as you please, and flipping pancakes—was a monster. And right beside him stood Meredith, happily squeezing oranges for juice.

Meredith's mother didn't know whether to laugh, cry, or scream for help. So she fainted.

Meredith placed a cool dishcloth on her mother's head. The monster fanned Meredith's mother with the pancake turner. Finally, Meredith's mother opened her eyes.

"Good morning," said the monster. "My name is Buzzle. What's yours?"

Meredith's mother tried to re-faint, but it didn't work. So she sat up. She looked at Meredith. She looked at Buzzle. "I think I need a cup of coffee," she said weakly.

"Coming right up," said Buzzle. "But first let's get you seated." Buzzle held the chair while Meredith's mother sat at the kitchen table. Then he shook out a fine linen napkin and laid it across her lap.

"My, my," said Meredith's mother, "you certainly are a gentle monster."

"And grateful too," said Buzzle.

Meredith's mother was puzzled. "Grateful?"

Buzzle poured her coffee. "Oh yes. Grateful to you for telling Meredith to make friends with me. I've always wanted a friend." He poured pancake batter onto the griddle. "Will you be my friend, too?"

Meredith's mother didn't know what to say. Then she found the answer in the sizzling griddle. "If your pancakes are as good as they smell," she said, "You can count me in!"

The three new friends made breakfast last till dinnertime, for the pancakes were the best ever— and light as a dream.

When the Wizard Wished

By Trinka Enell

With a dazed shout, Herbert the bumbling wizard fell out of bed. "Graceful as always," cackled Mycroft, the crow, from his perch on the footboard.

Blushing, Herbert stood up. "I was having a nightmare," he told the crow. "I dreamed that millions and millions of people wanted me to use my magic to solve all their problems."

Mycroft pointed a wing out the tower window. "I hate to tell you this," he cawed, "but guess what? It wasn't a dream."

Tripping over his wizardly robe, Herbert stumbled to the window. A long line of people stretched from the tower door down the dusty road.

Herbert groaned. "There must be hundreds of them! Tailors, sailors, mail carriers, even a messenger from the King—all waiting for me to magically solve their problems."

Mycroft flapped to Herbert's shoulder. "You wanted to be a wizard," he said.

"Not anymore!" Herbert declared. He snatched up his magic wand and twirled until it glowed red. "I wish to be a tailor!" he shouted.

"A what?" squawked Mycroft. "Wait!"

But there they were—in a small, quiet shop, with bolts of cloth piled around them. In the center of the shop stood a cutting table. Beside it stood a rack for scissors, needles, and thread.

Before they had a chance to see more, someone pounded on the door. "My first customer!" Herbert said in delight. Straightening his wizardly hat, he threw open the door. In stomped a huge bear. "I'm here for my winter coat!" the bear bellowed.

"W-w-winter coat?" Herbert repeated. He looked around the room. There, on the cutting table in pieces, lay an immense fur coat.

"I'm afraid it isn't quite finished yet," Herbert told the bear.

"*WHAT?*" roared the bear.

Mycroft moaned and hid his head under his wing.

"I'll finish it within the hour," Herbert promised. Grabbing a sleeve piece, he began to sew as fast as he could.

"You'd better!" bellowed the bear. He tromped out the door.

An hour later Herbert held the finished coat up to the light for inspection. "Oh no!" he said. "I sewed it inside out!"

Heavy footsteps sounded outside the door. "Now we're in for it!" Mycroft squawked. He dove under the cutting table.

Herbert scuttled after him. "What do I do now?" he cried.

"Don't ask me," Mycroft croaked, "you're the one who wanted to be a tailor."

"Not anymore!" said Herbert. Yanking out his wand, he twirled until it glowed red. Just as the door burst open, he shouted, "I wish to be a sailor!"

And there they were—on a gently rocking sailing ship. A warm sun shone down and a cool breeze ruffled the sails.

"Perfect!" Herbert exclaimed.

Mycroft fluttered to the railing. "Perfect? What about pirates? And sea sickness, and—"

Herbert just laughed. "I can handle any of that,"

he said. Whistling, he found a mop and began to swab the deck.

A short time later Herbert noticed that the sky was growing dark. "Hah!" Mycroft said, flying to Herbert's shoulder. "Handle this!"

Herbert looked up. Roiling black clouds filled the sky. Lightning flashed and thunder boomed. Rain pelted down. Then, WHAM! An enormous wave smashed into the side of the ship. Herbert and Mycroft tumbled across the deck and splashed into the heaving sea.

Flailing his arms wildly, Herbert snatched out his wand. A wave smashed it from his hand. "Mycroft!" Herbert cried, "get my wand. I can't swim!"

"Now that's a surprise," Mycroft cackled. He dove into the ocean, caught the wand, and thrust it at the wizard. "Dry land!" he said. "Hurry!"

Herbert whirled the wand furiously. He shouted into the wind, "I wish to be a mail carrier!"

And there they were—strolling down a shadowy forest path. Herbert had a mailsack slung over his shoulder.

"Now this is the life!" said Herbert. "Birds singing, bees buzzing, and not a single king, bear, or sea storm to bother us."

Mycroft flapped tiredly to the top of the sack. "Yeah?" he muttered, "how do you feel about ogres?"

Herbert stared. Across the path, a battered mailbox leaned against a vine-covered cave. The name on the mailbox read "Ollie Ogre."

"I'm sure he's a perfectly nice fellow," Herbert said stiffly.

"Yeah, right," Mycroft croaked. He zoomed to the nearest tree. Just as he tried to vanish in the leaves, a fang-toothed ogre thundered from the cave.

"Got my package yet?" he roared.

Herbert gulped. He dumped the contents of the mail bag on the ground and pawed through them. "I'm afraid not," he said.

The ogre's face turned purple. "I want my package, and I want it now!" He loomed over Herbert.

Herbert yelped and yanked out his wand. "Forget magic!" Mycroft cawed, zipping down from his tree. "Run!"

Whirling, Herbert ran. He kept running until he reached a flowering meadow, far from the ogre's cave. Then he slumped against a log and tried to catch his breath. "I don't think I want to be a mail carrier, either," he gasped.

Mycroft dropped to Herbert's shoulder. "How about that!" he cackled. "So, what do you want to be? Really?"

"Really?" Herbert repeated. "I don't know, but this time I'd better think more carefully."

Then Herbert smiled. He jumped up, took out his wand and twirled until it glowed red. "I wish to be a wizard!" he shouted. He grinned at Mycroft. "**A vacationing** wizard!"

And there they were. . . .

LORD LOUDERMORE'S VISIT

By Marianne Mitchell

"Oh, dear!" sighed King Goodwin. "Lord Loudermore is coming for a visit. He's hardly my favorite person." King Goodwin stared at the letter in his hand. It read:

In order to learn more about your kingdom, I am sending my ambassador, Lord Loudermore, to visit you. Please be nice to him.

King Timothy

King Goodwin pulled the velvet cord that hung beside his throne. In moments, his faithful friend, Jester, appeared.

"Sire," he said, removing his three-cornered hat and bowing low.

"We have a real task ahead of us, Jester. Lord Loudermore is coming to visit."

"Oh my, that will be nice!"

"Nice? We're the ones who have to be nice. He arrives tomorrow, so we should get the castle ready." With another low bow, Jester disappeared.

Early the next morning, a golden coach pulled by six white horses arrived at the castle. Lord Loudermore climbed out, brushed the dust from his puffy sleeves, and gave his feathered hat a shake.

"Welcome, Lord Loudermore!" King Goodwin said. "I hope you had a nice trip."

"But of course, my dear King. My coach rides as smoothly as a cloud across the sky."

"Oh my," Jester said. "How very nice!"

"Come. Let us show you around," the king said.

The king and Jester took Lord Loudermore to the top of the castle tower. "From here you can see all the lands of my kingdom," King Goodwin said proudly.

"Hmm, yes" mused Lord Loudermore. "But of course, our towers are so tall, they disappear into the beautiful, shimmering clouds. Why, we can't even see our kingdom!"

"Oh my, that sounds nice!" Jester said.

Next, they took Lord Loudermore for a ride in the countryside. As their horses clattered out the castle gate, Lord Loudermore looked down into the small river that flowed under the bridge.

"Is this your moat?" he asked.

"I suppose you could call it that. My subjects like to come and fish along the banks. Sometimes I even join them," the king said.

"Well," huffed Lord Loudermore, "the moat around our castle is so deep that sea monsters have come to live there."

"Oh my," Jester said. "That sounds nice."

The king, Lord Loudermore, and Jester galloped across the fields until they came to a quiet lake. When they stopped their horses, a rabbit leaped out of the brush and scampered away.

"What was that?" Lord Loudermore asked.

"Oh, that was just a country rabbit," said the king.

"Ha!" Lord Loudermore exclaimed, slapping Jester on the back. "Why, where I come from the rabbits grow as big as cows, and they give milk, too!"

"Oh my," Jester said. "That sounds nice!"

Jester got the picnic basket and spread out a lunch of chocolate cake, roast beef sandwiches, fried chicken, macaroni and cheese, and seven other yummy courses. Lord Loudermore cleaned his plate and then asked for seconds.

"Nice little snack," he said, patting his tummy. "We have snacks just like this right before every meal back home."

"Oh," Jester said with a sigh. "That sounds nice."

Lord Loudermore stretched out under a tree and closed his eyes. Soon he was fast asleep and snoring. King Goodwin took Jester aside for a private talk.

"I'm getting tired of all his bragging," the king said. "Isn't there any way to stop him?"

"I believe, Sire," Jester said, "that I'll find the answer right here by the lake."

Jester went for a walk along the lake shore. Soon he came back with two giant turtles. He carefully placed them on the belly of the sleeping Lord Loudermore. It wasn't long before Lord Loudermore stirred, opened his eyes, and then screamed, "Help! Help! Get these monsters off me!"

King Goodwin and Jester each grabbed a turtle and helped Lord Loudermore get up.

"Now, now, your lordship," Jester said with a smile. "You mustn't be afraid. These are only the tiny fleas of our kingdom."

"But of course, your fleas must be much bigger," the king said.

"Fleas? Oh, no! Nothing is *that* big!" Lord Loudermore jumped on his horse and galloped back to his own land. He didn't even say good-bye or take his golden coach.

"Well," King Goodwin said with a smile. "Maybe one thing that fellow learned is that bigger isn't always better."

"Oh my," Jester said. "That *does* sound nice!"

Roses are Orange, Violets are Brown

By Janet S. Anderson

One morning at breakfast, Allie looked at her juice. It was green. Spinach green. "Oh, no," she said. "What's Chroma mad about this time?"

Her mother peered over her brown newspaper. "Old Mr. Dunbar is complaining that the sky isn't as blue as it used to be. Chroma wants him to take it back and say he's sorry."

Allie knew Mr. Dunbar. "He'll never take it back. And today is picture day at school. My new peach dress is probably purple with black dots."

It was brown. Everything in Allie's closet was muddy, chocolate brown.

"I feel like a worm," Allie said. "I feel like a blob of gravy."

"You look fine," her mother said. "But red lights are blue today, and green lights are orange. Be careful at the corner."

"Red lights blue, green lights orange," Allie muttered on her way down the street, trying to ignore the yellow grass and the purple trees. "Or is it red lights orange?"

Nobody else could remember, either. At the corner, cars were piled up in confusion. Horns beeped. Drivers shouted. The guard, her hair hot pink under a neon-green hat, looked embarrassed as she waved Allie across.

"Cotton candy," she said. "I look like cotton candy with a pickle on top. Don't bother hurrying to school. The principal woke up with a blue-striped nose, and school's delayed until he can figure out how to cover it up."

"Good," said Allie. "That gives me time to visit Chroma. Maybe I can talk her into changing things back to normal."

"Be careful, honey," the cotton-candy guard said. "When the mayor went to see her this morning, she turned him orange. He looks a sight."

He did. The mayor was in the town square, kneeling in front of an old man sitting on a bench. His Honor looked like a squashed tangerine. "No!" the old man was shouting, his teeth flashing from gold to yellow to purple. "No, no, no, no, NEVER!"

So much for Mr. Dunbar saying he's sorry, Allie thought to herself.

It wasn't hard to find Chroma. Her white house was surrounded by a white fence. Chroma herself was standing out front, dressed in a long white robe. Her white hair was frizzled around her head. She was scowling.

"What an ugly dress," she said. "Go away."

"Please," Allie said. "It wouldn't be ugly if it was the color it's supposed to be."

"Supposed to be?" Chroma shouted. "Do you know how boring that is? I'm in charge of color." She kicked the grass. "But grass is only 'supposed to be' green." She kicked a tree. "Bark is only 'supposed to be' brown!" She kicked her white fence. "And everything of mine is 'supposed to be' white, white, white until the end of time."

"Why?" Allie said.

"Don't you know anything? Because my name, Chroma, means 'color.' All color, all the colors together. And the only color that's made up of all the colors is white! Boring, boring white!"

37

"Please," Allie said. "Don't get angry, but we just did colors in science. I know about all the colors in white light because we separated them with a prism. We made the most beautiful rainbows. Paint colors are different. When we mixed all the paint colors together, we got black." She backed away. "Please. That's what happened."

"Black?" Chroma burst into tears. "A black dress? A black house? Everything black, forever and ever?"

"But why?" Allie said. "If Chroma means color, why can't you have *all* the colors, all different every day? Why not?"

"Oh, no," said Chroma. "I wouldn't dare. Something bad might happen. Something might turn me into a toaster. Or a watermelon."

"Why?" Allie said once more. She took a deep breath. "Look. Just try. Make this fence post . . . red. If you feel yourself bulging out or burning toast, you can turn me . . . lima bean green."

Chroma thought. "No, Brussels-sprout green."

Allie took another breath. "I'll risk it if you will."

Without warning, the fence post glowed bright red. Chroma clutched Allie and gasped. "Do you see any seeds yet? Any rind?"

"Of course not," Allie said. "Try the other."

"Blue," Chroma said. "Pretty! But what about me? Do you see any bagels popping out of my head?"

"No bagels," said Allie. "There never will be. 'Chroma' means *all* the colors."

"Why, everybody knows that," Chroma said. She twirled around. "Oh, I can't wait. Everything I own will be a different color every day. Exciting colors. Wonderful colors! Look! Look!" Her dress rippled like a rainbow.

"It's beautiful," Allie said. "But Chroma, listen. With all your exciting colors, you don't want to bother with our boring ones. Couldn't we just have them back? Then you could forget us."

Chroma was making her house turn from blue to purple and back again. She waved an impatient hand. "I guess so. Who cares? I have more important things to think about now."

As Allie ran happily back through town, she saw Mr. Dunbar still sitting on his bench. He was squinting up at the sky, which was now a deep azure. "I still say it's not as blue as it used to be," he grumbled.

"Take it back!" came a shout from the direction of Chroma's house.

"I will not!" Mr. Dunbar shouted back.

Allie looked at Mr. Dunbar and started to giggle. He had been turned into the most beautiful shade of sky blue she had ever seen.

You Can Tell a Nice Dragon

By Judith A. Enderle

Draco, the young dragon, sat in the corner of the cave. His eyes widened. Occasional puffs of smoke drifted from his nose. He was into the best part of his book.

Mama dragon sighed. Papa dragon frowned. "Draco, tomorrow is the day you leave to find your place in the world. Why aren't you practicing your roaring, swooping, and flame-throwing?"

Draco looked up. "Papa, I don't like to roar, swoop, or throw flames. I like to read."

Papa snorted. "No roaring, no swooping, no flame throwing? How will you ever find a place in the world?"

"Don't worry, Papa," soothed Mama. "Draco will be fine. There is a place for everyone in the world."

Mama turned to Draco. "You'd better go to bed, sweetheart," she said. "You should leave early."

The next morning, Draco happily ate 104 charcoal pancakes for breakfast. He hummed a tune as he packed his toothbrush, his books, and a spare pack of matches (in case his fire went out). Then Draco kissed his mother and father goodbye and set off.

As he approached the first village, he called out, "Do you have a place . . .?"

"A dragon! Hide!" the people shouted. They ran. They didn't listen to Draco.

At the second village, they slammed and locked their doors before Draco even opened his mouth. "Papa would be proud," Draco said, "but I am very sad. Everyone is afraid of me."

He headed into the mountains.

At noon, Draco stopped to rest. Far below, he could see another small village. "I can't face anymore shouting or slamming doors," he said sadly. Draco curled up, closed his eyes, and went to sleep in the shadow of the mountain.

"Brubbadubb, grubbadubb," muttered Draco in his sleep as something tickled him. Slowly he opened his eyes.

"Wake up, dragon." A tiny boy with red hair was pulling on one of Draco's ears. Carefully, so as not to hurt the boy, Draco stretched. "Who are you?" he asked.

"I'm Tony," he said.

"A pleasure to meet you, Tony," Draco said politely. "I'm Draco, the dragon." He waited for the boy to yell or run. Instead, Tony sat down near him.

"How do you do, Draco," he said.

"Aren't you afraid of me?" Draco asked.

"No. You look like a nice dragon," Tony replied.

"How can you tell I'm a nice dragon?"

"Because nice dragons have friendly eyes and kind smiles."

Draco tried to see if he had a kind smile.

"Why do you have a suitcase?" Tony asked.

"To carry my books," Draco said.

"You're fooling me. Dragons can't read."

"I can," Draco said. He dumped his suitcase out on the ground.

"Oh, you have some good stories. These are some of my favorites, too." Tony helped Draco repack his suitcase.

"Are you from these mountains?" Tony asked.

"No. I'm making my way in the world. It's very hard, you know." He sighed. "I don't think everyone knows about dragons with friendly eyes and kind smiles."

"I know just the place for you," Tony said. "Come with me." He grabbed hold of Draco and pulled him down the mountain.

At first, the villagers shouted and slammed doors. Draco felt very sad. Then, one by one, they came out again.

"What a sight!" the butcher cried. "Will your Papa let you keep him?" the baker joked. The villagers laughed as Draco and Tony passed.

Tony walked on. Draco followed along. Farther back, the villagers followed.

At the far side of the village, Tony stopped. "You wait here," he told Draco. He skipped up the walk to a tall building.

Moments later, Tony reappeared with a round, wrinkled elf of a man. The man pulled his spectacles down from his polished forehead and peered through them at Draco. "My!" he said. "A real smiling, friendly-eyed dragon. Why did you bring him to me, little one?"

"Draco, show Mr. Nosco how well you read," Tony said.

Draco took a book from his suitcase. He cleared his throat, opened to the first page, and began: "Once upon a time . . ."

Tony interrupted, "And look how tall Draco is, Mr. Nosco."

"I see," Mr. Nosco said.

"What does he see, Tony?" Draco asked.

"You read well and you are tall," said Tony. "Mr. Nosco is our librarian. He needs an assistant to read to the little children and to reach the books on the highest shelves. You could do both, Draco."

"Only if you want to, dragon!" exclaimed the friendly librarian.

"Oh, I would like to try." Draco said happily. "I love to read and I'm sure I can reach the highest shelf in your library. Also, I'd be glad to help keep the library warm in the winter." He blew a perfect smoke ring.

"Then, Draco the dragon, I hereby name you first assistant librarian," Mr. Nosco said.

"Welcome, welcome!" cried the villagers as Draco followed Mr. Nosco and Tony up the library path. Draco grinned. He had found his place in the world.

Princess Ramey's Royal Recital

By Betty Porter

One day Princess Ramey heard a beautiful sound floating in through the palace window. It was like gulls swooping in the sea breeze. It changed to cymbals crashing in a brass band. Then the music whispered a lullaby.

"What is that sound?" asked Princess Ramey.

No one knew.

Madam Forte, the court musician, was called in.

"That is Lord Allegro, my prize piano student," she said proudly.

"I wish I could play the piano like Lord Allegro," Princess Ramey said.

"But you haven't finished the moat you started around the castle," the King exclaimed. "It's turned to mud, and your little brothers and sisters keep tracking dirt into the castle."

"And what about your class in crown decoration?" the Queen asked. "You should finish little Prince Hamilton's crown before the next parade."

"I'm tired of moats and crowns," said Princess Ramey. "I want to play the piano like Lord Allegro."

The King stroked his beard. "I suppose you could try it," he said.

The Queen sighed. "But you must promise to stay with it, dear. Your dragon hunting lasted only a week, and you haven't even unpacked the hot-air balloon kit yet."

"I know I could play the piano if I had lessons," said Princess Ramey.

So Madame Forte came to the palace for Princess Ramey's piano lessons.

"You must practice every day," Madame said.

"I want to swoop like the gulls, crash like cymbals, and whisper a lullaby," replied Princess Ramey. "I do not want to practice."

Princess Ramey sat at the Royal Grand Piano. She fiddled. She twiddled. She trilled. She wiggled.

She sighed. She groaned. She stared out the window and hummed. But she didn't practice.

A few weeks later Princess Ramey said, "It's time for my first recital."

Madame Forte raised her eyebrows. "Are you sure you're ready?"

"I know I could play if I had an audience," Princess Ramey answered.

On the day of the recital everyone gathered in the Royal Ballroom. Princess Ramey swirled onto the stage in her yellow taffeta skirt and landed with a swish on the piano bench. Her fingers fumbled for the keys. A strange sound rumbled out of the Royal Grand.

Princess Ramey bit her lip. She tried again. The sounds were shrill and squawking. Princess Ramey winced. She turned to the audience.

"My first piece is a duet," she said. "Would Lord Allegro please help me?"

Lord Allegro jumped up from his velvet chair. He stumbled over a footstool and tripped on the stairs to the stage. When he reached the Royal Grand, his feet got tangled in Princess Ramey's taffeta skirt. He fell in a heap at her feet.

"Please excuse Lord Allegro," Princess Ramey said, helping him up. "He's a little nervous."

Lord Allegro and Princess Ramey sat down at

the keyboard. She nodded for him to begin. Lord Allegro's fingers swooped. They crashed. They whispered. Princess Ramey picked out the melody with one finger.

As the last chord drifted away, the audience was silent. Then the King began to clap. The Queen smiled and blew kisses. The applause crescendoed into a roar.

Princess Ramey and Lord Allegro held hands and bowed.

"You are wonderful, Princess Ramey," the king said.

"Lord Allegro is the one who can really play," answered Princess Ramey. She turned to the blushing boy. "Will you play duets with me every day? If I practice very hard, maybe I can swoop and crash and whisper at the piano the way you do."

Lord Allegro nodded and grinned.

"Then we will give a REALLY royal recital!" said Princess Ramey with a wink.

A Dinosaur Day

By Ellen Leroe

Danny loved dinosaurs. He loved everything about them. He ate *Tyrannosaurus Rex*-shaped cookies, washed his face with dinosaur egg soap, and slept beneath an *Apatosaurus* blanket.

"Someday you'll turn into a dinosaur yourself, if you don't watch out!" his father said one evening when Danny refused to eat the tuna casserole his mother made for dinner.

"I want a stegoburger from the Fossil City Cafe!" Danny demanded.

"I want you to quiet down," Danny's father said, "or you won't go to the museum tomorrow." Danny ate his tuna casserole.

The next morning was his class trip to the dinosaur exhibit. Danny woke up and felt funny.

He threw off his *Apatosaurus* blanket and put on his furry slippers with the *Pterandon* wings. He marched into the bathroom and began to brush his teeth with the *Triceratops*-shaped toothbrush. When he looked in the mirror, he shouted in surprise. His teeth looked like *Tyrannosaurus* teeth, all pointy and long like pencils.

His mother called him to breakfast. Danny was scared to open his mouth when he drank his juice, but all his mother said was, "Are those new teeth coming in, dear?"

Danny ate his breakfast of cereal and toast, but it tasted bad. He thought the large roast thawing on the kitchen counter looked much tastier.

"Don't forget to take your lunch today," Danny's mother said. "I made your favorite, peanut butter and jellyapterus."

On the way out the door, Danny's hands began tingling. There were big scales covering his fingers. "I'm glad you're wearing your gloves," Danny's mother said. "It's cold out there." She smiled and gave him a kiss.

Danny walked to the school bus. He wondered what all his friends would say when they saw he was turning into a huge dinosaur. Everyone was too excited about the trip to the dinosaur exhibit to notice anything different.

The bus came. Danny got on, but his new long tail got caught in the door. "Oh, Danny, your green scarf is dragging," said the bus driver.

Danny was the last one to get off the bus. He walked on all fours into Mrs. Wilber's class. He thought his best friend Michael or the other kids would say something, but no one did.

Danny had to sit in the very back of the classroom. He had gotten so large that his head stuck out the window and his tail stuck out the door. He took up the entire back row.

"Is everybody ready for the trip to the dinosaur exhibit?" Mrs. Wilber asked. "Everyone pick a partner and line up at the door."

"Hey, Danny, will you be my partner on the trip?" Michael turned around to ask.

Danny tried to say yes, but his voice came out in a roar. *Now everyone will notice,* he thought.

"Danny, stop whispering," Mrs. Wilber said.

Danny got up to get in line and all the chairs fell over. His long tail knocked down the bookcase. For the first time, Danny felt scared.

"Mrs. Wilber, I don't feel well," Danny said. His words came out like thunder. Mrs. Wilber felt his forehead and frowned. "You do look a little green."

Danny ran home on all fours. His mother put him to bed and called the doctor.

The doctor took Danny's temperature and poked and prodded him. The thermometer snapped in two between Danny's sharp, pointy teeth. *Now someone will see that I'm a dinosaur,* he thought. But the doctor only sighed and called Danny's mother into the room.

"What does Danny have?" asked Danny's mother.

The doctor shook his head. "He's suffering from a bad case of *Brachiosaurus* Burnout. I've seen it before. Take two dinosaur toys away from the boy every hour on the hour and call me in the morning if he isn't better."

The doctor left. Danny's mother tiptoed around the bedroom. She took down the *Plesiosaur* mobile over the bed and the three-foot skeleton of *Edaphosaurus* near the closet.

Danny lay under the blanket very quietly. His tail snaked out the door like a green vacuum cleaner. He didn't care if he ever saw another dinosaur again in his life.

All afternoon his mother came in to check on him. She took his windup *Stegosaurus* one time, his *Triceratops* lamp the next. She removed the giant *T. rex* poster from behind the bed. Pretty soon the room was dinosaur free. There was not one single dinosaur toy, book, slipper, or decal left.

Danny felt better. He didn't feel strange anymore. He was no longer a dinosaur. When his parents called him to dinner, he felt hungry.

"Look what I brought the sick boy," Danny's father said. "*Pterodactyl* pizza from the Fossil City Cafe!"

"My favorite!" Danny cried, forgetting his day.

When he reached for a slice, his fingers began tingling. "Uh, no thanks," Danny said. "Don't we have any of that tuna casserole from last night?"

The Troll
Wedding

By Marianne Mitchell

Way up north in the mountains of Norway, a young lass named Karla sat fishing from a rock in the middle of a river. Karla didn't notice the tiny red eyes that watched her from the forest. She didn't notice the hairy troll that climbed up the rock behind her.

"Whatcha doing?" asked the troll.

Karla almost jumped into the water, she was so surprised.

"Who are you?" she asked.

"Uff-da," replied the troll. "You're not from around here, I can tell. You don't have a tail."

Sure enough, Karla noticed that Uff-da had something that looked like a cow's tail wagging and dragging behind him.

"You're not human, I can tell. What are you?"

"I'm a troll, of course. And you're sitting on our special rock."

"What makes it so special?"

"All of our important events happen on this rock. Today my daughter Ugla is getting married right here."

"On a rock?"

"Of course. We make a wedding bridge first. You come to the party, *ja?*" Uff-da grabbed Karla's arm and whisked her across the water and into the forest.

"I must be dreaming all this," mumbled Karla to herself. But she didn't want to make the troll angry. An angry troll might use his magic to turn her into something slimy, like a frog.

Uff-da led Karla deeper into the dark forest. The pine trees were so thick that only a little sun filtered through their branches. "Too much sun for a wedding!" said the troll. He hopped on his left foot and muttered something in troll-speak. Suddenly the forest got darker. A cold wind blew through the trees, and snow fell everywhere.

Karla's teeth chattered. "You want it cold and snowy?" she asked, pulling her sweater tighter.

"Best for a wedding. Everything is white!"

Next, Uff-da took Karla to the cave where Ugla was getting ready for her big day. They watched as dozens of lady trolls fussed over the bride. One lady troll combed Ugla's snarly hair into a lovely green blob. "However did you decide to marry Alfi?" she asked.

"Oh, there were several fellows who crawled out from their rocks to court me. But I was very picky," Ugla said. "I made them all go through many difficult tests."

"What kind of tests?" another friend asked, handing Ugla a broken mirror.

"First, I made a big pot of moldy mushroom stew. And the messiest eater was my Alfi!"

"Wonderful! What was the next test?" another troll lady asked.

"The mushroom stew made those boys very tired. So they stretched out on the ground and soon were fast asleep, snoring like pigs. And my Alfi was the loudest!"

"You lucky girl! Then what?" her friends asked.

"While they were all asleep, I sniffed the toes of each fellow. And my Alfi's toes were the stinkiest!" said Ugla.

"Oh, what a clever troll you are!" they cried.

It seemed to Karla that trolls had very different ideas of what was proper. But she kept quiet. Maybe if she was polite they'd let her go home.

Uff-da then took her to another part of the forest where cook trolls were busy making the wedding cake. They mixed in two dozen rotten eggs; a gallon of sour milk; and twenty scoops of crunchy flour, full of bugs. When it was all done, they whipped up a frosting of dark green pond scum.

"Isn't that lovely?" said Uff-da.

Karla nodded and gulped, hoping she wouldn't have to eat any of it. Just then, a sound like mooing cows filled the air.

"Ah, the wedding chimes!" said Uff-da. "Time to begin." Trolls jumped out from every tree and rock and scrambled to a clearing. The cook trolls pushed the wedding cake to the center. On the count of ONE! everybody grabbed a handful of cake and shoved it into their mouths. Next, they filled their mugs with fishy river water.

"*Skoal,* to Ugla and Alfi!" they shouted.

At last it was time for the ceremony. The trolls wiped their mouths on their sleeves and pushed their way into line.

"Hear Ye! Make way for the bride and groom!" someone shouted.

Ugla glowed like a firefly, waddling beside the groom. Alfi grinned a toothless smile and nodded to all he saw. Behind them came Uff-da, plunking out a polka on his tail. The Official Joiner was next in line, and the rest of the trolls followed.

When they reached the river's edge, Karla noticed that a delicate bridge of twigs had been built over to the special rock.

The Joiner led the trolls onto the bridge. "Like a bridge joins two sides, let us join these two," he said. The twiggy bridge swayed back and forth. Karla stayed behind. She didn't want to risk adding her weight to the bridge.

The Joiner chanted the wedding words to Ugla and Alfi. "Mo ho du leva! Hundra, hundra or!" Then he tied their tails together.

"Hoo-hah! Hoo-hah!" shouted the trolls. They clapped their furry hands and stomped their even furrier feet. Someone pushed Karla into the crowd to meet the happy couple. It was too much for the little bridge. The twigs snapped, dumping everyone into the freezing river.

"What a fun wedding!" the trolls yelled. They bounced out of the icy water and scampered off into the trees.

Shivering, Karla crawled back up onto the rock. Uff-da was standing on the river's edge, waving his arms at the sky. The sun came out and all the snow disappeared.

"I told you it was a special rock," said Uff-da.

"Did all this really happen?" asked Karla.

"Would I pull your tail?" said the troll.

"But I don't have a tail."

"Exactly!" And with that, the little troll tumbled like a ball into the dark forest.

One Wish

By Carolyn Bowman

"Aunt Jenny, you're here!"

"Every last particle of me," she said, swinging her carpetbag through the front door.

I hugged her and Mom and Dad hugged her, because Aunt Jenny is the best. The places she goes and the stories she tells about her travels are better than going to the movies. And the surprises!

"What did you bring?"

"Paige Simpson!" said Mom, "hold your horses. Give Jenny a chance to land."

Aunt Jenny winked at me. "I don't think you'll be disappointed."

But I had to wait—for a very long time. My parents and Aunt Jenny had a lot of catching up to do. Aunt Jenny's work as a buyer for an antiques company takes her all over the world, and they had to hear every last detail of her most recent trip to Morocco before they were willing to give the two of us a chance to be alone.

Finally, Mom and Dad went into the kitchen to start dinner, and Aunt Jenny dropped her carpetbag on the coffee table in the living room. Then, spreading her arms, she pretended to be a jet. "Whew! I feel like I'm still at thirty thousand feet."

She even looked like a bird as she hovered over the carpetbag, waving her hands. But I loved her excitement. She was like a little kid as she said, "Now for your surprise."

She opened the carpetbag, and I strained to see inside, thinking of other surprises she'd brought me. My favorite was the rug from Bangladesh— the one that was supposed to fly. It didn't, but I never told.

"Ta-da!" she said, and lifted out a glass ball on a black wooden stand. Putting it on the table, she hunched over it, weaving her fingers around it. "I found this in Casablanca, in the Old Medina."

"Medina? What's that?" I asked.

"It's a shopping center made of tents. Vehicular traffic is mostly camels and goats, but the bargains and the haggling—*oo-la-laaa!*"

For most kids this would need a translation. But Jenny is my aunt, so I knew. Haggling is the way people in some countries decide what an item should cost. The seller suggests one price, and the buyer suggests a lower one. That is only the beginning. Knowing Aunt Jenny, she would always get a good price.

"What does it do?" I asked, reaching out to touch the glass ball.

"Be careful," she said, patting my hand. "In that bit of crystal are all the secrets and spirits of time. You wouldn't want to shake them up."

The ball looked like those you see at Christmastime, filled with scenes blanketed in loose-flying snow. Only this one was empty and solid.

"It's a wishing machine," Aunt Jenny said. "One wish per customer."

"Huh?"

She closed her eyes. Then, putting her hands on the glass, she started humming.

"What's going on?"

"I'm making *my* wish." Opening one eye, she said, "You don't mind, do you?"

"Oh, no. Go right ahead." Anyone else would think my aunt was, well, a little weird. But she's not, and she was being very serious.

I waited until she finished, then I hugged her. "Oh, Aunt Jenny, I'm so glad you're here."

"There you go," she said. "One wish—signed, sealed, and delivered. What a find!" She nodded at the crystal ball.

I was shocked. "You wished for a *hug?*"

"More or less." There was a twinkle in my aunt's eye as she gave me my present.

"You wasted your one-and-only wish on a hug? But I give you those for free."

Aunt Jenny shrugged. "I guess people wish for what matters most to them."

I held the glass up to the window and it cast a rainbow on the wall. "It's beautiful," I said.

"And waiting for your wish," Aunt Jenny replied.

I spent the afternoon thinking about everything I had ever wanted. The list grew so long, I had to write things down. It included: to play my trombone better than Peter Haskell, the big brag; to finally make the basketball team; to get a chemistry set (the fancy kind with everything in it); to make better grades; to be a millionaire. Still, I couldn't decide.

I heard Dad singing. Going downstairs, I saw him and Aunt Jenny setting the supper table. Mom came in from the kitchen, and the three danced around the room, laughing and talking.

Suddenly, I knew my wish. It was so clear I nearly fell as I rushed back upstairs to the crystal ball. I wrapped my hands around it, closed my eyes, and said the words.

Nothing miraculous happened. No puffs of green smoke billowed, and the ball didn't warm to my touch. But I felt warm inside, just hoping.

Later, at the table, Dad said, "Let's join hands." I took Aunt Jenny's and Mom's hands and felt a squeeze from both.

"Paige," Dad said, "Jenny's going to spend a part of the summer in Spain. How would you like to go with her?"

He could have said *the moon* for all I cared. It was true! The crystal ball *did* work. I leaned close to Aunt Jenny and said, "That was my wish—to go with you."

"One secret per customer at this table," Mom said with a smile.

Aunt Jenny grinned and said something that shocked me right to my toes. "The trip was decided on last month, and we agreed to keep it for a surprise. You haven't used your wish. Back to the drawing board, Paige!"

CHRISTOPHER MEETS COLUMBUS

By Lois Breitmeyer and Gladys Leithauser

At the kitchen table, Christopher sprinkled a thick layer of cinnamon sugar on a slice of bread and butter. He took a big bite.

The room was quiet. The clock ticked on the wall. The soup simmered on the stove. Sun streamed through the window and made a bright circle on the table.

Christopher picked up the jar and poured a wiggly row of cinnamon sugar around the circle of golden light . . . .

"Stop that!" cried a shrill little voice. "You're wasting my spice!"

Christopher blinked. A tiny man in peaked hat and high boots hopped from a chair to the table.

"I'm Sir Cinnamon," he said. "And you're very careless, Christopher. Obviously, you don't know the true value of cinnamon."

"You're an elf," gasped Christopher. "I'm sorry! I love cinnamon, honest. Cinnamon cookies and candy and sticky buns. Applesauce . . ."

"Problem is, you take spices for granted," the tiny man said. "Once upon a time brave people risked their lives to find them. To prove it, I'm taking you on the greatest spice search ever. Over five hundred years ago, in 1492."

"You mean Christopher Columbus, don't you? Will I see him?"

"Absolutely." The elf stamped his boot three times. The kitchen—and Christopher with it—began to whirl like a top. They went faster and faster, then—

THUD! Christopher was standing on the deck of a wooden ship. Sails billowed overhead and huge waves slapped the sides of the sturdy vessel.

"Ouch!" Something pinched Christopher's ear. He turned his head. Sir Cinnamon was sitting on his shoulder.

"This ship is the *Santa Maria*," the elf said. He pointed at a bearded man sitting on a coil of rope, deep in thought, studying a map. "There's the great explorer himself."

"Hello, Mr. Columbus!" Christopher said, but the man didn't look up.

"He can't hear or see you," Sir Cinnamon said. "You're invisible."

Christopher looked over the explorer's shoulder. "That map doesn't have America on it!" Christopher exclaimed. Then he remembered. "Of course! Columbus hasn't discovered America yet. Right?"

"Yes." The elf chuckled. "That's where this ship is headed, but Columbus doesn't know that. He's sure he's sailing to the islands of the Indies, where wonderful spices grow."

"I don't get it," Christopher said. "I thought Columbus was looking for a 'New World.'"

"No!" the tiny man said. "Spices! Don't you understand? Spices are more precious than jewels. Pepper, cloves, nutmeg, but especially *my* wonderful spice, cinnamon!"

"No offense," Christopher said, "but *why?*"

"Remember, this is 1492. No refrigerators. Spices help preserve meat and fish. And spices make old food taste better."

"Rotten food! Yuck." Christopher choked.

"Spices are used as medicines, too," Sir Cinnamon said. "When these sailors get sick—stomachache, fever, headache—they try to heal themselves with different spices."

Christopher nodded. "They didn't have medicines like aspirin or penicillin . . . Well, one thing, though. They didn't have to have shots."

A rough-looking sailor was steering the ship with a big wooden wheel. "Captain Columbus," he called. "The crew is restless. We haven't seen land for many weeks. Lots of the men are sick. They groan about wormy bread and briny water. Some are talking mutiny if you don't turn back!"

"We set forth to reach the spice lands," Columbus shouted at his crew. "We must keep going. Sail on!"

That night the moon was bright. Most of the sailors were asleep on the deck. Suddenly, a cry rang out from the sailor on watch. "LAND HO!" he shouted. "LAND HO!"

Everyone jumped up and began to cheer. "Men," Columbus shouted, holding a spyglass to his eyes. "We've done it! This must be an island of the Indies. We'll call the natives *Indians*."

"Amazing!" Christopher gasped. "They don't know they've discovered America. Please," he begged Sir Cinnamon, "I want to meet Christopher Columbus. Can I? Pleeeeze!"

"Well . . ." The tiny man hesitated. "I don't usually use that power, but just this once—"

Christopher looked down. He was wearing black knickers, a scratchy wool shirt, and heavy shoes. Columbus himself was standing right in front of him.

"Congratulations, Captain!" Christopher said.

Columbus looked down and smiled. "Thank you, son. You must be one of the cabin boys. Yes, this is a great day! People will remember October 12, 1492, long after we're dead."

Christopher nodded. "Long after *you're* dead. That's right, sir."

"What's your name, son?"

"Christopher."

"Good name, eh?"

"The greatest, sir."

Columbus turned away and peered through the spyglass again. The shoreline and trees stood out against the night sky. Christopher gazed at the orange moon gliding over the new land. The moon slowly slid behind the horizon, and Christopher closed his eyes.

Sun streamed through the window. The clock ticked on the wall. The soup simmered on the stove. Christopher was at his kitchen table again. Sir Cinnamon had vanished.

"Wow, what a wonderful dream!" Christopher exclaimed. He picked up his slice of bread; there was one bite gone. Then he saw the cinnamon sugar he had sprinkled in a wiggly circle on the table. He leaned forward, hardly able to believe his eyes. The cinnamon sugar had changed into neat little letters.

He read out loud: GOODBYE, CHRISTOPHER. DON'T FORGET ME.

Ever so carefully, Christopher spooned up the cinnamon sugar and put it back into the jar.

The Dragon Tooth

By Trinka Enell

One morning Laurie found a large jagged rock beneath a rosebush. "Look, Daddy! A dragon tooth!" she cried.

Her father examined the tooth. "Looks like a rock to me."

"Oh no," Laurie said, "it's a dragon tooth. A special dragon tooth. When I plant it, a baby dragon will grow. You'll see."

"Well," Laurie's father said with a grin, "don't forget to keep it watered!"

"I won't," Laurie answered. And she didn't. Every day for three weeks Laurie watered the tooth, watched, and waited.

Finally, one morning as the sun warmed the dirt, the ground burst open and a small, scaly head popped out. A baby dragon cried "Meep! Meep!"

"Hello," Laurie said. "I bet you're hungry!" Gently, she scooped up the baby dragon and carried him into the kitchen. "Do you like peanut butter cookies?" she asked.

"Meep!" answered the dragon. He ate four, one right after the other. Then—his tummy as round as a golf ball—the baby dragon fell asleep cradled snugly in Laurie's arms.

Tiptoeing upstairs, Laurie laid the sleeping dragon on her pillow and ran outside to find her father.

"Daddy!" she hollered, when she saw him weeding in the vegetable garden, "the baby dragon finally hatched!"

"Baby dragon?" her father said.

"Remember—the one that grew from the dragon tooth I found!" Laurie said.

"Oh, *that* dragon!" her father nodded. "Well, I hope you can keep it fed, Laurie. I'm sure baby dragons eat a lot!"

Laurie's father was right. When the baby dragon woke up, he ate three more cookies, a piece of toast, two hard-boiled eggs, and a big hunk of cheddar cheese. And he was still hungry!

In desperation, Laurie offered him some broccoli. The baby dragon took one bite, then spit it out— all over Laurie's bedspread.

"Don't be messy," Laurie scolded, "or Daddy won't let you eat at the table when you're big."

The little dragon looked at the mess on the bedspread. He hung his head. "Meep . . ." he said sadly.

Laurie hugged him. "That's all right," she said. "I made messes when I was little, too. You'll grow out of it." A happy "meep" came from the dragon, and he hugged Laurie back.

That evening at dinner, Laurie wrapped a slice of meat loaf and a baked potato in a paper towel. "An after-dinner snack?" asked her father.

"No, it's for my dragon," Laurie said.

"Your dragon? Oh, I forgot about him! Here, take the rest of my meat loaf, it'll help fill him up! But remember, growing dragons need vegetables."

Laurie frowned. "He won't eat broccoli," she said.

"Try carrots," he advised. "All babies like carrots."

"Thanks Daddy, I will!" Smiling, Laurie hurried into the kitchen, scrubbed four carrots, then carried everything upstairs.

"Daddy says baby dragons need vegetables," she told the little dragon, when he'd finished his meat loaf and baked potato. "So here are some carrots. Make sure you eat them all!"

"Meep!" said the dragon. He gobbled the carrots, then settled down beside Laurie for a story.

Three days later the baby dragon was so tall his head reached Laurie's chin. "I think you're big enough to eat at the table now," Laurie said, "if you want to go down for breakfast."

"Meep! Meep!" said the dragon.

Laurie's father was in the kitchen making coffee when Laurie and her dragon sat down at the big table in the dining room.

"Now remember," Laurie said, dividing her scrambled eggs and bacon with the dragon, "eat neatly!"

"Meep!" replied the dragon. And he gobbled his bacon and eggs very neatly. Then, before Laurie could stop him, he lunged across the table and started to gobble her father's bacon and eggs.

"Stop!" Laurie screeched.

Her father rushed in from the kitchen. "Oh my gosh!" he gasped, "It's real! A real, live dragon!" He slid to the floor in a faint.

Meeping anxiously, the little dragon leaped off the table. He dashed over to Laurie's father and rasped a warm, wet tongue across his cheek.

Laurie's father's eyes blinked open. He gazed up at the dragon. He groaned.

"Daddy?" Laurie said, "are you all right?" My dragon was really worried about you!"

"He was?" Her father sat up and looked more closely at the small dragon. He smiled. "That was nice of him."

"He's a nice dragon," Laurie said.

"Meep!" said the dragon.

Then Laurie's father frowned. "But Laurie, how do you intend to keep feeding him?"

"Plant more vegetables," Laurie said. "He loves vegetables now—except for broccoli. He can even help dig! He can earn his food by doing other chores, too, like weeding and raking leaves in the fall."

Her father chuckled. "I imagine he could," he agreed. He stood up and patted the dragon softly on the head.

"Well, young dragon, it looks like you have a home. But if you're going to eat at the table, you have to use proper table manners. Agreed?"

"Meep!" said the dragon. "Meep! Meep!"

And from that day on, he did.

A Palace
for the
Princess

By Ruth A. Sakri

Once upon a time there was a very spoiled princess. She always wanted her own way—right away. Usually she was such a nuisance that she got what she wanted.

One spring day the princess went to see the court wizard. "You can do all kinds of magical things," she said. "So you must do some magic for me. I want a special new palace."

But the wizard was very wise. That's why he was a wizard. "You have a beautiful palace," he said.

"The birds are singing like flutes and the wild-flowers are blooming like rainbows. You should be happy there. Besides, I am very busy now. I am helping a poor woodcutter get rid of an evil witch's spell."

"I don't care about the woodcutter," pouted the princess. And she flounced away angrily.

One summer day the princess went to see the wizard again. "*Now* are you ready to create a special new palace for me?" she demanded. I must have a new palace immediately.

"Your palace is beautiful," said the wizard. "The swans are floating on the lake like clouds and the mountain breezes are like pure perfume. You should be happy there. Besides, I am busy teaching a good fairy to help a blind boy."

"I don't care about the blind boy," grumbled the princess. And she tossed her head and strode away very angrily.

One autumn day the princess went to see the wizard once again. "Do it now!" she snapped. "Create a special new palace for me!"

"Your palace is beautiful," sighed the wizard. "The trees are colored like jewels and the ripe fruit is sweet with dew. You should be happy there. Besides, I am busy driving away a dragon that is frightening a whole town."

"I don't care about the whole town!" cried the princess. And she stuck out her tongue and stamped away very, very angrily.

One winter day the princess went to see the wizard a final time. "This time you will do as I tell you," she sneered. "If not, my father will fire you."

The wizard looked into her eyes for a long time. Then he said, "You shall have what you want. Just what is it?"

The princess smirked. "I want a wonderful crystal palace," she said. "I want it to sparkle like my eyes and shine like my hair. I want a palace after my own heart."

The wizard cocked a bushy eyebrow at her and said, "If that is what you want, then you shall have it." Without even saying thank you, the princess stomped away.

A few days later, the wizard went to see the princess. "Your palace is finished," he said. "Come, I will show you."

It was truly a wonderful palace. It sparkled like diamonds and shone like stars. "You have exactly what you wanted," said the wizard. And he was right, of course. That's why he was a wizard. The shiny and sparkly palace and everything in it were made entirely of snow and ice. It was indeed a palace after the princess's own heart.

The Adventure
of Roland
the Royal Storyteller

By Mike Cunningham

Roland was the best storyteller in the land. He had begun telling stories at an early age to amuse himself, since he was an only child. In time he became very famous.

He was so famous that one day the king sent Roland a very important request. It said:

"Will you move into my castle and become the Royal Storyteller?"

Roland quickly said, "Yes!" He packed his bags and moved into the Royal Palace.

Now Roland became even more famous. People visiting from other lands listened to Roland's stories and tried to tell them again when they went home. But no one could tell Roland's stories as well as Roland himself.

Roland told wonderful stories like "The Dragon Who Burned Himself Up," "Bruin, the Loyal Bear," and (Roland's favorite) "Prince Falston and the Elves' Treasure." So Roland, a simple, honest man, became very popular, very rich, and very famous. This made one person in the kingdom very jealous.

Theona, the evil witch, had once been the king's favorite storyteller before her evil ways forced the king to exile her to the Forgotten Forest. News of Roland's fame reached Theona in her exile, and she vowed to take revenge on the king's new Royal Storyteller.

Disguising herself as a seamstress, Theona left to search for Roland. She found him in a garden near a lake. "Oh, Royal Storyteller," Theona began. "I have traveled hundreds of miles to hear one of your stories. Would you tell me one?"

Roland was always happy to tell a story, even if his audience was only one person. So he began, "Once upon a time . . ."

Theona was soon so interested in his clever tale of knights and knaves that she nearly forgot why she had been looking for him. When his wonderful story ended, she remembered. When he wasn't looking, Theona secretly cast an evil spell on poor Roland. Then she thanked him for his story and returned to Forgotten Forest.

That evening after supper, Roland was asked to tell a new story to the king and his guests. "Once upon a time," Roland began confidently. He started to describe how a land once woke up in darkness and how the people searched for and brought back the sun. *Quite a good story,* Roland thought to himself as the story unfolded. But that is not what everyone else thought.

One by one the ladies and gentlemen around the table began to fall asleep. At first Roland thought they were simply tired from their long journeys. Soon everyone except the king was fast asleep, and Roland knew that something was very wrong. Finally, the king himself nodded off. Roland sadly went to his own chambers for the night.

The next day Roland was again asked to tell a story, but the same thing happened to his audience. The king was angry. The people were frustrated. Roland was very worried. He went to a wise doctor in the village to ask for help.

When Roland described what had happened, the doctor said, "Roland, my boy, this sounds like a spell to me. If it is, only one person could have done it. Theona, the former Royal Storyteller, who lives in exile."

The doctor was right, of course, so there was nothing he could do with medicines or potions to help Roland's problem. Then Roland had an idea. He put on a sailor's blue uniform and slipped into the Forgotten Forest to find Theona.

After searching for nearly a week, Roland spied a small cottage built in the shadows of an overhanging cliff. Boldly, he approached the cottage and knocked loudly on the door. Inside the noise startled Theona, who never had visitors. People in Forgotten Forest were just that, forgotten. Slowly, she opened the door. *A sailor? Here?!* she thought. She did not recognize Roland as the storyteller.

"Who are you? What do you want? How did you find this cottage?" she asked.

Theona's questions were just what Roland expected. His answer was ready.

"Though I do not appear so, I am a prince, sent on a long and perilous journey," Roland explained. "I am to prove my valor so that I may marry the daughter of my king. Three treasures are the objects of my search. May I tell you more?"

Theona yawned, but asked the stranger to continue. So Roland told a tale more marvelous and mysterious than any that had ever crossed his lips. And as he talked, Theona's eyes grew heavy. Soon, right there on her doorstep, the evil witch fell asleep, caught in her very own spell.

Roland came straight back to the castle and requested the opportunity to tell one more story before being banished for his failures. The king was willing to allow it, since Roland was, after all, his favorite storyteller.

Roland told the king the story of his adventure in Forgotten Forest. He told how Theona had cast a spell on his stories, but that he had found Theona and used the spell against her. Now she was sound asleep in her cottage under the overhanging cliff, and the spell she had cast on Roland was broken.

"A fine story indeed, lad," said the king. "But how do you know the spell is broken?"

"Because, dear king," Roland answered with a smile, "You are not asleep!"

Abracadab-Rabbit

By Anita Borgo

Wade could ask his best friend, Alex, to trade lunches when Mom made ham salad, and he would do it.

Alex could ask Wade to walk his pet poodle that had the silly haircut, and he would do it.

Wade could ask Alex anything—almost. What Wade couldn't ask Alex to do was to help him with basketball. Wade stunk at basketball, and he was embarrassed to ask for help.

Most recesses he pretended he couldn't play because he hurt his foot or sprained his wrist. Instead, he'd watch Alex slam dunk and wonder how he could do it. Today recess was canceled because of an assembly. The Great Belini and his rabbit, Elmo, performed magic tricks.

"How do you think the Great Belini pulled Elmo out of his hat?" Wade asked Alex as they trudged home after school. Wade shifted his backpack to his other shoulder. The pack seemed heavier and the walk home longer today.

Alex said, "Pulling a rabbit out of a hat is the oldest trick around. Millions of years ago caveman magicians pulled prehistoric rabbits out of Stone Age hats. What's magic is the way you added fractions in math. I wish I could do that trick."

"Fractions are a cinch." Wade lowered his backpack to the grass. "Wait up. I've got to move some books around." When he unzipped his pack, a pair of honey-colored ears poked out. There was no mistaking that twitchy nose.

"Elmo?" Wade and Alex said together.

Wade scooped up the rabbit. "How'd you get in there?" Elmo twitched his nose again.

Alex thought someone played a trick on Belini by hiding Elmo. Wade decided to call the principal, Mrs. Collins, when he got home.

"Want to practice shooting baskets later?" Wade asked. He hoped Alex might show him how to slam dunk.

Alex shook his head. "I have math homework."

Wade scratched Elmo's head as he watched Alex walk away. "If only I could play basketball like Alex." The rabbit twitched his nose and wiggled his ears in return.

Wade slung the backpack onto his shoulder and hurried home. Maybe if he practiced running, he'd be quicker on the court. He held Elmo tightly. His walk turned into a jog. His jog became a run. He sprinted the last block and jumped over his mother's peony bushes. His feet felt tingly.

"Wade, that's quite a leap." Mom stood on the front porch holding a paintbrush. "Who's that?"

"Elmo. He belongs to Mr. Belini. Somehow he got into my backpack."

"That must be why Mr. Belini called. He'll be here in an hour." Mom stretched to paint a spot above the doorway, but it was out of reach. "I need a ladder."

"Let me try." Wade handed Elmo to Mom and took the brush. He jumped up and dabbed the spot.

"Wade, how'd you reach so high?"

"Just jumped." His fingers felt itchy. Wade traded the brush for Elmo and walked around the back.

Next door, Lori Johnson practiced free throws in her driveway. "Hey, Wade want to play?" she called as she tried a lay-up shot.

He was about to fake a sprained toe, but today he felt like playing. They found a cardboard box for Elmo and placed him on the back porch.

Wade bounced the ball twice. It didn't feel large and awkward like it usually did. It felt like part of his own hand. He dribbled quickly toward the hoop, floated upward, and slam dunked.

"How did you do that?" Lori exclaimed.

"I don't know," Wade said. "I just did it. Sometimes it happens in math class. I know the answers to problems without working them out. It's never happened in basketball."

"Do it again," Lori said. They counted twenty-eight straight baskets before Wade went home to do his homework.

Wade carried Elmo upstairs to his room. "You brought me luck," Wade whispered to the rabbit as he put Elmo on the floor. Elmo scooted under the bed. He peeked out from under a blanket and watched Wade open his math book.

Adding mixed fractions was a snap; he didn't understand why Alex thought it was so hard. He wrote out the first problem, but forgot to line up the numbers. He wadded the paper and made a perfect basket into the trash. On the second problem, he forgot to find common denominators. Before long, his trash can overflowed with wads of crumpled paper.

"Wade, Mr. Belini is here," Mom called.

Elmo scampered to the door. Wade snatched up the rabbit and went downstairs.

"Elmo, I've missed you tremendously." Mr. Belini wore his cape and top hat from the show. "Has he been a good rabbit?"

"He's been no trouble at all to take care of. He just sat quietly," Wade answered.

"Yes, that's not usually a problem." Belini stared at Wade. "However, has he been good? Are things as they should be?"

"Um, well, something strange *did* happen this afternoon," Wade said. He explained about basketball and math.

Mr. Belini rubbed his chin. "When you found Elmo, did he twitch his nose and wiggle his ears?" the magician asked.

"Don't most rabbits?" Wade replied.

"Yes, but Elmo isn't like most rabbits," Mr. Belini said. Elmo is more like my partner than a rabbit."

"You mean Elmo's a magician, and he turned me into an athlete?" Wade laughed. "There's no such thing as real magic."

"Believe what you will," Mr. Belini said, turning toward the door.

Wade stopped him. "But what does basketball have to do with math?"

"There is balance in magic," Mr. Belini said. "Something is given easily, and something else is taken away."

Wade thought about his homework. "How do I make it go back?"

"Magic fades. By tomorrow, things will return to the way they should be." Mr. Belini swooped out the door with Elmo.

Wade thought about the trash can full of wadded homework. He called Alex. "I need help with basketball, and if you want, I'll help you with math."

"Just like that? You'll learn slam dunking, and I'll learn fractions?" Alex asked.

"No, not just like that," Wade replied. "With practice and a little help, you'll understand fractions, and I'll get better at basketball. Working together is the trick." Wade smiled to himself as he and Alex made plans. He knew friendship was a magic that wouldn't fade.